At the Center of
the World

At the Center of the World

Based on Papago and Pima Myths

By BETTY BAKER

Illustrated by MURRAY TINKELMAN

347717

Macmillan Publishing Co., Inc.
New York

Collier Macmillan Publishers
London

Macmillan Publishing Co., Inc.,
866 Third Avenue, New York, N.Y. 10022
Collier-Macmillan Canada Ltd., Toronto, Ontario
Library of Congress catalog card number: 72–88820
Printed in the United States of America

10 9 8 7 6 5 4 3 2 1

Library of Congress Cataloging in Publication Data

Baker, Betty.
  At the center of the world.
  CONTENTS: Earth magician.—Coyote drowns the world.—
The killing pot.—[etc.]
  1. Papago Indians—Legends—Juvenile literature. 2. Pima
Indians—Legends—Juvenile literature. [1. Papago Indians—
Legends. 2. Pima Indians—Legends. 3. Indians of North
America—Legends.]
I. Tinkelman, Murray, illus. II. Title.
PZ8.1.B1724At   299'.7   72–88820   ISBN 0–02–708290–3

Contents

At the Center of
the World

1

Earth Magician

Dark was all. There was no moon, no sun, no stars. But the dark hid nothing, for there was no earth.

Then the darkness began to gather. Slowly, slowly, it turned on itself, coiling deeper than dark, working power and magic. Until out of the deep and heavy dark came Earth Magician.

He drifted alone, a man of power, a great magician. He floated in darkness with nothing to see, no one to hear.

"But I need not drift forever," he said.

With his magic stick he scraped dust from his chest and rolled it into a ball. He patted it flat, wide as his hand. He patted it flatter, patted it wide. Flatter and wider, wider and flat, until he could stand. When he could stand, he danced. He danced it flatter, stamped it wide. Round and smooth he danced the world.

He had a place to sit and walk but it was still dark.

Earth Magician poured water from the magic stick. He mixed clay and shaped it into a water jar. He filled the jar with water and breathed upon it. The water froze. Earth Magician broke the jar and threw the ball of ice into the sky. There it stayed, moving east to west, giving light and warmth. But when Sun moved west to east through the Underworld, there was dark.

Earth Magician made another bowl and filled it with water. Again he breathed a ball of ice and threw it into the sky. It followed Sun from east to west, then west to east, lighting the night.

But Moon was a woman. Often she covered part of her face. Sometimes she would not look down at all. Then nights were dark.

Earth Magician filled his mouth with water and blew it hard against the dark sky. The drops froze and stuck, making stars.

There was a place to sit and walk and light to see.

"But still I am alone," said Earth Magician.

He took the shadow from his left eye and from it molded Buzzard, a bird with wings of power.

"Look!" cried Earth Magician. "See what I can do! I made Moon, Sun and stars. I shaped the world."

Buzzard said, "Why did you make it flat? There is nothing for me to look down at."

The great bird rose to the sky, swooped and rose again, his wing tips cutting mountains and rivers, canyons and mesas.

"That is good," said Earth Magician. "You can help shape plants and animals."

Buzzard pretended not to hear. All day he floated in the sky, dark as a shadow, admiring his mountains and rivers.

Alone Earth Magician mixed clay and molded plants. Mesquite and cactus, corn and grass, melon, squash and beans, all plants giving food and seeds he shaped. He tapped each plant with his magic stick to give it life.

He molded birds and little animals, eagle and thrush, woodpecker and wren, lizard and snake, ground squirrel and rabbit. And large animals, deer and mountain sheep, cougar and peccary. Each he tapped with the magic stick, each was given life. Then Earth Magician shaped the first people.

He made them short and very strong. They did not sicken, they did not die. Babies were born. They grew and had babies who grew and had babies. No one died but everyone ate. They ate beans and melons, seeds and cactus. They ate birds and lizards, snakes and leaves.

"There isn't a bush or animal left," said Buzzard. "I see nothing but dirt. They must eat that or each other."

"It was a mistake not to let them die," said Earth Magician.

He hooked the magic stick over the edge of the sky and pulled it down, crushing people, animals, plants and mountains. The stick made a hole in the sky. Earth Magician squeezed through it, into the Second World, pulling Moon, Sun, stars and Buzzard after him.

Again Buzzard cut mountains and rivers. Again Earth Magician mixed clay, molded plants and birds and animals. When he made the second people, he let them grow old and die. But young women and men turned gray and died. Then boys and girls grew gray and stooped. Soon babies turned gray when they were born.

"You still don't have it right," said Buzzard.

"I will try again," said Earth Magician, and he pulled down the sky.

Again he escaped through a hole in the sky, taking Sun, Moon, stars and Buzzard with him.

Again Earth Magician shaped plants, making new kinds, making trees to shade the rivers Buzzard cut. He made more birds and animals and his people grew old and died at the proper time. Earth Magician was pleased.

Then the third people began to smoke. First only old men smoked as they sat in shade or sun. Then young men left the hunt and the fields to sit and smoke. Soon boys and babies in cradleboards had reed and cornhusk cigarettes.

"There is smoke everywhere," complained Buzzard. "The world might as well be flat for all I can see of it."

Earth Magician sighed. "I must do it all again."

Again he pulled down the sky and took Sun, Moon, stars and Buzzard through the hole made by the magic stick. Again Buzzard cut mesas and mountains, rivers and canyons, shaping the world to please himself. Again Earth Magician mixed clay and molded plants, animals and birds.

"You're still making mistakes," said Buzzard. "The lizards' legs are too short and the snakes have none at all."

"I am tired," said Earth Magician. "I need someone to help."

"I'll keep watch for someone," said Buzzard and flapped up to drift in the sky.

On top of a mesa he saw Coyote, child of Moon and Sun. Moon was too busy to tend her child and had left him under a bush. Coyote sat on the mesa, crying for his mother.

"Come with me," said Buzzard.

On the way to Earth Magician they met Eetoi, son of Earth and Sky, with the power of both.

"Come with us," said Coyote.

"It is for me to ask," said Buzzard. "Come with us, Eetoi."

Buzzard led them to Earth Magician and said, "I bring Eetoi and Coyote to help you."

Coyote looked at the animals and said, "You made the legs too fast. They will be hard to catch."

Eetoi said, "The people are crooked. Some have only one arm or leg. How can they run or shoot bows?"

"Do not anger him," warned Buzzard. "When he is angry he pulls down the sky. Three times he has pulled it down. We barely escaped through a hole in the sky."

"If he pulls it down again," said Coyote, "can I escape with you?"

Buzzard laughed. "You cannot even reach your mother. How will you jump through a hole in the sky?"

Coyote worried and watched the sky, crying his fear to his mother at night.

2

Coyote Drowns the World

One sunrise Coyote went to Earth Magician. He said, "I dreamed the world filled with water."

"No! No!" cried Earth Magician.

Coyote told him, "Water poured from under stones, over mountains and out of trees. Water covered the world and reached the sky."

"You have told your dream," said Earth Magician. "I tried to stop you but you told it. Now it will happen."

Buzzard hurried to spread the news.

Coyote went to ask Eetoi, "How will you escape?"

Eetoi said, "I will make a great water jar, crawl inside and seal the mouth. It will float upon the water."

"Will you take me with you?"

"Of course," said Eetoi.

Coyote told Earth Magician and added, "There will not be room for you."

"I will float on my magic stick," said Earth Magician.

Day and night clouds thickened and grayed, shutting away the stars, Moon and Sun. Water streamed from under rocks, flowed from canyons and spouted from the tips of bushes and trees.

Lizards, snakes and animals ran to Eetoi. He let them into his red clay jar. When Coyote came splashing through the puddles, there was room for only Eetoi. Coyote raised his nose and howled.

"Do not cry," said Eetoi. "Crawl into my flute. It will hold you on top of the water."

Coyote sank to his belly. He squeezed and wriggled, wriggled and squirmed. He squeezed himself small and the flute large until all of him fit except his tail.

Eetoi crept into the jar. He stuffed the opening with cornhusks and plastered them over with clay.

Water covered the bushes. It rose over the trees. The people fled to Crooked Mountain. Halfway up they climbed.

When the water wet their feet, they climbed higher.

The flute drifted by, Coyote's tail held high. The water rose and the people climbed.

The water jar floated past, slowly turning. The water rose, the people climbed. They climbed until they clung to the top of Crooked Mountain. The water reached their knees but they could climb no farther.

Earth Magician drifted past, saw them and heard their weeping. Raising his left hand, he turned the people to stone. The water covered them. Earth Magician could see nothing but water, the flute and jar upon the water and the birds above it.

Buzzard swooped back and forth, searching for a place to make a hole in the sky. But the clouds were too heavy, he could find no sky. He hung upside down from the clouds and waited. The other birds crowded between clouds and water, fluttering and weeping.

"When the water meets the sky, we will die," cried the thrasher.

"We will die. We will die," repeated the mockingbird.

With bill and claw, birds clung to the clouds and wept.

"You sound like Coyote," said Buzzard. "And your tears only add to the trouble."

"Yes," said the cactus wren. "Stop crying. If we must die, let us die singing."

Softly, with many beats of silence, he began to sing. The mockingbird joined his song, then the thrasher. Soon all the birds, feebly and with hiccups, were singing.

The water stopped rising.

"It is magic!" cried Buzzard. "Your song is magic. Sing!"

Puffing their breasts, the birds sang. The water lowered. There was room for Buzzard to fly.

"Sing!" he cried. "Your song has power."

Stronger came the birds' song. The top of Crooked Mountain appeared.

"The magic is working," said Buzzard. "Sing!"

The birds were tired but they sang. Foothills appeared and the edges of canyons.

"Just a few more songs," pleaded Buzzard. "Don't stop now."

The birds were weary. Their necks were limp and their tongues hung out but they sang. They sang until the water was back in the riverbeds and the world was dry.

Eetoi opened the water jar and pulled Coyote out of the flute. Earth Magician climbed down from a cliff, carrying the magic stick.

"See what I can do?" said Buzzard. "I saved the world!"

"You are a bird of power," said Eetoi.

"It was a song of power," said Earth Magician. "And now I must make people again."

"I will make them," said Coyote. "I am very clever. My people will be better than any ever made."

He mixed clay and began to mold.

"I never made people like that," said Earth Magician.

"I said they'd be better than yours," said Coyote.

Eetoi said, "How can they run with webs between their toes? How can they shoot bows with webs between their fingers?"

"I told you I was clever. With webbed hands, they can drink water without carrying a bowl. And if the world is drowned again, they can paddle around in safety."

Four times Coyote barked over his people. At the fourth bark, they came to life and waddled to the river, otter, geese, beaver and duck, all things that live in water.

"I will make the people," said Earth Magician. "I have made them many times. I know how."

Eetoi said nothing. He built a hut and mixed his clay where no one could watch. From Earth, his mother, he shaped his people, old and young, children and babies. When all were formed, he set them outside under Sky, his father. There Eetoi's people came to life. They were strong and handsome with long black hair. They could run and dance, talk and hunt.

Earth Magician watched them and was angry.

"You have let them talk," he said. "That is a mistake."

"If they talk, they can sing," said Eetoi. "They will sing of Earth Magician and tell how he shaped the world."

But the song the people sang was of Eetoi, how he shaped them from red earth and gave them life.

Earth Magician raged. "A mistake! A mistake!"

He hooked the magic stick on the edge of the sky.

"He's pulling down the sky," warned Buzzard.

Coyote yelped and ran in circles.

Eetoi rushed to save his people. He struggled with Earth Magician, wrestling and pushing until the magic stick slipped and the sky snapped shut.

With a roar of anger, Earth Magician sank into the ground.

"Stay," said Eetoi. "We will work together."

Earth Magician sank lower and faster. Eetoi grasped his arms, trying to hold him, but Earth Magician sank and disappeared forever from the upper world, leaving his angry sweat on Eetoi's hands. When Eetoi shook off the droplets, disease and sickness came into the world.

Alone, Eetoi cared for his people. He gave them words of power, songs of magic, songs for growing corn and curing illness, ways of calling rain. All things they learned from Eetoi and they built their villages near him at the center of the world.

3

The Killing Pot

During corn-planting season a strange bird appeared in the village at Gray Mountain, a green bird with heavy beak and grasping claws.

It swooped on the children, beating and tearing at their heads and arms. They ran to the cooking shelters but the bird followed, screeching and attacking the women.

Some fought the bird with firewood. Others fled into the houses. One woman stayed by her cookpot, feeding the fire, boiling the water.

16

The bird swept down upon her. The woman ducked and the bird tumbled into the pot. The woman scooped out the dead bird, plucked its bright green feathers and returned to her grinding stone.

The pot continued to boil. Higher and faster it bubbled and plopped, higher than the pot edge, high as a child's head. Spouts of green broth rose and turned and splashed at the woman's feet.

She went to her mother and said, "The pot is trying to burn me."

"The bird was evil," said her mother. "You must spill the broth."

The woman found a long stick to push over the pot but when she crept near, the broth bubbled higher, the splashes flew wider. She tried to surprise the pot but always it knew she was there.

Women and children gathered to watch, moving away when the broth splashed wider.

"The pot has no fire," they wondered. "Yet the broth does not cool."

"I will add water," said the woman.

She set a jar on her head ring and went to the spring. When she returned, the pot still bubbled. The woman rushed close as she dared and threw the water at the pot.

Much spilled down the sides of the pot and onto the ground but some of the water fell inside.

Green broth rose straight from the pot. Higher than her head it rose, steaming and gurgling. Four times the woman carried water from the spring. Four times the broth spouted in anger.

The fourth time it reached the shelter roof. The branches burst into flames. Broth and sparks flew to other shelters, setting them all afire.

The men came running from the fields. Green broth splashed to meet them, burning and scalding, holding them back. They heard their families weeping in the mud houses but could not reach them. Those inside dared not come out.

Coyote passed after sunset and caught a new scent, the smell of strange food cooking. He heard men and women calling to each other.

"The village is having a dance," he said.

Tail high and tongue dripping, he went to join the feast. But he found no dancers, no men with rattles and basket drums. The cooking shelters were gone. The only cookpot boiled too fiercely to approach though there was no fire beneath it.

Behind the houses where the green broth could not

splash, the men were holding council. Coyote sat among the elders and was told about the pot.

"You must kill it," Coyote advised.

"We have tried," said the headman. "We cannot reach it."

"Then you must leave the village."

"We will not go while our families live," said the men. "And our families cannot leave the houses."

"Then you must send for Eetoi," Coyote told them.

The headman said, "It is far to his home on Baboquivari. Before a messenger returns with Eetoi, children will die of thirst."

"I could take your message and return tomorrow," Coyote told him. "I am child of Moon and Sun."

"Take our message," said the headman. "Ask Eetoi to help us. Tell him when the pot is killed, we will make a new dance."

Coyote decided. "I will go."

The men worried. "You will return with Eetoi tomorrow?"

"Did I not come through the flood in Eetoi's flute?" Coyote answered.

He called to his mother. She lighted the way until he passed Black Mountain. On he went, not stopping to hunt, but he did not reach Baboquivari until the sky lightened. He climbed the mountain, up and around, searching for

Eetoi's cave. When he found it, Sun was rising. Eetoi bathed in the pool by the door.

"Brother," said Coyote, "I have come to ask your help."

While Eetoi dried and brushed his hair, Coyote told of the strange green bird and the killing pot.

"But you need not leave your home and pool," Coyote told him. "I will go. Teach me the words of power and I will kill the pot for you."

"They are my people," said Eetoi. "I am the one who will go."

"The way is long," said Coyote, "and Sun is hot."

"My people ask for my help," said Eetoi. "I must go."

He bound his hair at the back of his neck and painted the part red. Then he took up his shield and war club and went to help his people.

Coyote ran beside him, feet sore and belly empty. Half the day passed with no hunting but Coyote thought of the dance and feast to come and ran on.

The elders met them outside the village. The pot still bubbled and splashed. The women and children were still in the houses and had no water.

"I can save your families," Eetoi told them, "if Coyote will help. He must run to the door of the farthest house."

"That is the other side of the pot," said Coyote. "The broth will splash me."

"I will give you a song," said Eetoi. "You must sing it as you run."

"Will it save me from being burned?"

"No," Eetoi told him. "But it will make the pot angry. It may not notice when I attack. I may get close enough to kill it."

"Let us wait until dark," said Coyote.

"Our families need water," said the men.

"I must kill the pot now," said Eetoi. "Child of Sun and Moon, will you help?"

Coyote said nothing but he took Eetoi's song. He sang it as he leaped by the pot. Broth splashed over him. He yelped and snapped as it burned but he reached the door to the house.

Eetoi rushed at the pot. Once, twice, four times his war club struck the clay. The pot broke.

An old woman and her grandson rushed from the house where Coyote lay. Before the green broth seeped in the ground, they scooped up the liquid and drank. Their bodies thickened, hair grew. Brown bear and black bear stood in their places. They dropped to four feet and padded away to the mountains.

Coyote did not join the feasting. The hair had been burned from his back and tail. Blisters began to form.

Healers gathered, chanting their songs, blowing smoke. Eight nights they sang over Coyote's burns. The blisters dried, pain crept away.

Women tended and fed Coyote. Boys brought him rabbits and ground squirrels. His belly grew round and fat. Men stopped at his mat and spoke with respect.

The burns healed but Coyote lingered until the last of his hair grew back.

4

The Monster Eagle

While Coyote waited to heal, he passed the days gambling with a young man called Vandai.

Vandai's field grew weeds. His bow was warped and dusty. The cookpot held only what his mother gathered, for Vandai thought more of the gaming sticks than he did of hunting and farming.

He was lucky, and after Coyote left, Vandai seldom lost. His mother's storeroom filled. His loincloth was of cotton.

His earrings of shell and turquoise reached below his shoulders. But Vandai had no friend.

He shared his good luck with no one. He showed no respect to the elders, took no part in ceremonies. When he looked for a wife, no man would give Vandai his daughter.

He began to hide by the spring, chasing young girls, causing fear and anger.

The headman spoke to Vandai but Vandai mocked him.

The council met. Four men were sent to Eetoi.

They took gifts of tobacco and cotton and told him of Vandai.

"He spreads bad feeling," they said. "There is no peace in our village."

"I will help," said Eetoi.

He went into his cave. He ground together herbs and eagle feathers. As he worked he sang, words of power, a song of magic.

He gave the powder to the eldest messenger.

"Have a young woman mix this with water," said Eetoi, "and give it to Vandai to drink."

The headman's niece was chosen. Her hair was long and shining, her tattoos freshly healed. She was given the powder and told what to do.

Her uncle left his spinning and joined the gamblers.

When it was Vandai's turn to throw, the headman called, "We are thirsty."

His niece answered, "I will bring fresh water."

She walked by, eyes down, the water jar on her head. She carried a bowl for dipping water. In it was Eetoi's powder.

Vandai watched her. He soon threw all unmarked sides and lost the sticks. He rose and followed the girl.

"You are thirsty," she said, and lifted the bowl, the water mixed with the powder.

Vandai quickly drank. He began to itch. Bumps rose on his skin. From the bumps grew feathers. Before Sun left the upper world, Vandai was an eagle-man.

At first he stayed near the village, learning to hunt and use his wings. When he'd eaten all of the village dogs, he was too large for a tree branch to hold him.

Men carried clubs. Small children were kept under shelter. Vandai flew to the mountains where hunting was easier. Larger he grew, and heavier. The cliffs crumbled under his weight. Then he began to hunt people.

Buzzard flew to Baboquivari.

"You made a mistake," he told Eetoi. "You're no better than Earth Magician."

Said Eetoi, "I did as my people asked. I rid them of Vandai."

"The eagle-man you made is worse. When he hunts, even I must hide."

"My people say nothing," said Eetoi.

"Vandai caught their messengers," said Buzzard. "The first were sent three seasons ago. Now the villages have lost too many men. They dare send no more."

Eetoi considered.

"This is a hungry time," said Buzzard. "I can hunt only after the monster feasts. Then he is sure to sleep. I will soon be too weak to get off the ground. Then Vandai will have me, like a rabbit."

Eetoi said nothing.

"Your people suffer, too," said Buzzard. "Soon none will be left."

"I must save them," said Eetoi. "In four days I will come to the mountain where Vandai lives."

Buzzard hurried to spread the news.

Across the desert came Eetoi. Like a warrior he came, to save his people. His hair was bound up, his eyes painted black. His arrows were tipped with quartz.

"There will be a sign," he told the people. "If a dust cloud covers the mountain, all is well. But if Earth shakes and Sky turns black, you will know I am killed."

Eetoi shot his arrows into the cliff, one above the other. The warheads struck deep, the arrows held firm, making a ladder.

Singing, Eetoi climbed. Up the cliff he went, to the top of the mountain. Above the clouds he climbed, to Vandai's cave.

A woman met him. She had been the first carried off but she had not been killed. Her hair was dull and tangled. Her bones showed through her skin.

In the back of the cave was a pile of dead men. Against one wall leaned a cradle frame. Wrapped in it was an eagle-baby, winged and feathered like Vandai.

The woman wept at seeing Eetoi.

"Vandai will kill you," she said. "He will soon return and there is no place to hide."

"He will not find me," said Eetoi. "When will he sleep?"

"Not until he feasts," she told him. "Not for many days, unless I sing. Sometimes he sleeps when I sing."

A shadow swept over the cave door.

"It is Vandai," said the woman.

"Try to make him sleep," said Eetoi. "And do not fear, whatever happens."

Eetoi changed into a fly, buzzed to the ceiling of the cave and crawled sideways into a crack.

Vandai filled the cave door. He looked from side to side, one eye at a time.

"I smell a man," he said.

"You smell all those dead ones you leave around," said the woman.

"Man here," said the eagle-baby. "Man here."

Vandai cocked his head. "What did he say?"

"It is only baby noise," said the woman. "You know he cannot talk."

"Man! Man," said the baby monster.

The woman picked him up.

"He is tired," she said. "I will sing until he sleeps."

Vandai hunched his wings and settled to rest. As the woman sang, his eyes closed, his breathing deepened. Three times the woman stopped singing and called his name. Three times Vandai opened his eyes. But the fourth time she called, he did not waken.

Eetoi flew down and took his own form. With war arrows he killed the monsters, father and son. He cut the head from Vandai's body.

"I need water," he told the woman.

She brought a bowl. Eetoi mixed Vandai's blood with the water and sprinkled it over the dead men with eagle feathers.

Those on top sprang up shouting, angry and ready to fight. They were Apaches. To protect his people, Eetoi sent the Apaches into the mountains to live.

Next he brought to life the Maricopas. No one could understand them so they went west to live.

Those on the bottom had been dead too long. They were faded and weak. They woke crying, unable to live like real people. Eetoi was filled with pity. He sent the white men across the sea where there were guns and wagons to amuse them.

At last all was done. Eetoi led the woman to the door of the cave and sang for the cliff to bend down. Slowly the mountainside moved, sliding them to the ground and closing the cave behind them.

A great cloud of dust rose. Eetoi's people saw it and prepared a welcome.

5

The Killing of Eetoi

Girls had their maidenhood ceremony, became mothers and grandmothers. The grandchildren grew and had children and the seasons passed, each as it should.

During the dry time, the painful moons, women walked far to get water. But during that time when no rain fell, the giant cactus flowered. Sun strengthened and burned. The cactus fruit ripened.

Morning and evening, women gathered the fruit. They

boiled the red pulp and strained it. Inside the Rain House, a man who knew how prepared the juice. Outside, the people danced.

Two nights the men and women danced, singing the songs Eetoi had taught them, helping the juice to ferment. When it was ready, the juice was brought out.

With songs and proper ceremony, the men began to drink. They drank until they were dizzy, drank until happily drunk. Each man drank his fill as he wished for Earth to drink hers. And clouds gathered.

Rain washed the mountains, flooded the land. Earth drank her fill and corn could be planted.

Men tended the fields and sang up the corn, using the words Eetoi had taught them. Harvests were gathered. Grass dried, cactus shrank and the painful time was near.

Yet always again the cactus bloomed and always after the ritual drinking, clouds appeared bringing rain. All was as it should be until Eetoi began to do wrong.

First there was grumbling, then unhappiness and fear. Leaders from every village met, telling the wrongs Eetoi had done, deciding what could be done.

"If a young man of our village is full of himself, we speak with him," said one. "If he mocks our words, we know what to do. We behave as if he is not there. He

quickly learns we must help and think of each other. If we do not, we cannot survive. But what do we do when the thoughtless one, the selfish one, is Eetoi?"

For twenty days they talked, deciding what could be done. Then they returned to their villages and held council with their people.

All agreed. A day was chosen. Time sticks were sent to the villages. Hot and dry, the marked days passed. Four by four, the men set out.

They met at Baboquivari, men from every village. Their hair was tied up, the parts painted red. Their eyes were banded with black.

During the night they sang and smoked with proper ceremony. At dawn they climbed the mountain. They brought no gifts, no cotton or tobacco. They carried knives and war clubs. All wore eagle feathers.

Eetoi lay by his pool, drying after his bath. The men stared at the water.

"Our springs are dry," they said.

The leader silenced them.

"What do you want this time?" asked Eetoi.

The leader said, "The elders of the villages met. I bring you their words."

Eetoi sighed.

"You come asking for a wife," the leader said. "You are given one. Soon you beat her and send her home. Then you ask for another. Seventeen wives you have had, all of them young and beautiful."

"All of them stupid and lazy," said Eetoi.

The men murmured in anger.

"You interrupt our ceremonies," said the leader. "You mock our songs and dances and they have no power."

"They are *my* songs and dances," said Eetoi.

The leader said, "You come to the maidenhood ceremonies. You dance too long with the maidens. You are too free with them. If the girls are not properly purified, the village will be struck by lightning."

Eetoi yawned and said, "I can protect my people."

"You don't," said the leader. "When the cactus juice fermented, you drank it all. We could not hold the ceremony. We had no way to pull down the clouds. We could not call the rain."

"I cannot help you," said Eetoi.

"We do not ask for help," the leader told him. "Your power has turned to evil. You have stopped the rain. Springs are dry, the river shrinks. Corn will not grow. Our women sift dust for seeds."

"You are killing us," said the men.

When there was silence, the leader spoke. "The council has said you must die."

Eetoi laughed.

The men sprang upon him, seized his hair and clubbed his head flat. Then they painted their faces black and began the journey home.

They did not speak or eat. They dared not scratch nor touch their hair. They had killed a person and were in danger of madness until they were properly purified.

At dawn Eetoi appeared in their camp, laughing and calling them women.

The men leaped upon him, slashing with knives. When Eetoi was dead, they scraped out a hole and buried him. Then they turned their faces homeward.

Eetoi rose from the ground. At dawn he appeared at their camp, mocking their power as warriors.

Again the men killed him. They scattered his flesh to the four directions. They pounded his bones to dust and cast it to the winds. Then they went on.

The four winds blew, gathering the pieces, collecting the dust. A column of red dust followed the warriors, whirling and dancing. At dawn Eetoi stood before them.

"You have no power to destroy me," he said. "Do not bother me again."

The men cleaned their faces and went home.

Elders from all the villages met.

"We will ask Buzzard to help," they decided. "He came with Earth Magician from the First World. He is older than Eetoi. His power must be stronger."

Buzzard said, "I do not know that I have power."

"Earth Magician formed you from the shadow of his eye," said the elders. "You must be a bird of power, a great magician."

The elders talked and flattered. They sang of Buzzard's power, how he helped to shape the world.

"Perhaps I do have power," said Buzzard, "but it may not be the proper kind."

"Help us," pleaded the elders. "Only your power can save us."

"I will help you," said Buzzard.

But he feared Eetoi and dared not try to kill him. All day and night he thought. When Sun returned, Buzzard hung low in the eastern sky to greet him.

"The people ask your help," he told Sun. "They fear Eetoi. His power has turned his heart bad."

Buzzard followed Sun, talking as they rose. He told how Eetoi mocked the dancers, how he broke the ceremonies.

"I have not seen these things," said Sun.

"They are done while you light the Underworld," said Buzzard. "His people fear him but have no power to destroy him. Only you have power great enough."

"It is true my power is great," said Sun. "See how everyone hides from me."

"Even Eetoi hides," said Buzzard.

When Sun began his downward journey, he was persuaded.

"I will help," he said. "Where is Eetoi?"

"In his cave," said Buzzard. "Shall I call him out?"

"No," said Sun. "There is no need."

He spit in the pool before Eetoi's cave. Steam rose, filling the cave, scalding Eetoi and smothering him.

"It is done," said Sun.

Buzzard swooped over the villages.

"Eetoi is dead," he announced. "Sun and I held council and Sun has killed him."

The people were content.

But when Sun neared the entrance to the Underworld, Eetoi was waiting.

"Take me to the Underworld," said Eetoi. "I must speak with Earth Magician."

Sun said, "That is not done."

"You killed me," said Eetoi. "Now you must pay me."

Moon rose while they argued.

"Take me with you to the Underworld," said Eetoi. "You could not destory me. Whose power is greater?"

"This day is too long," grumbled Sun. "I agree."

Eetoi climbed the spiderweb holding Earth and Sky together, the web that kept Earth from trembling. Sun took Eetoi from the web and carried him to the world below.

6

The First War

"I have come," said Eetoi.

"Go away," said Earth Magician. "I want no more of your help. All things are as they should be in this world."

All things were not as they were in the upper world. Mountains were not as high, rivers not so deep. Shadows were pale, the edges soft.

"Sun is weak," said Eetoi. "He feels as if he looks through mist."

Earth Magician said, "Here he rests and gathers strength for his journey in the world above."

"I, too, must gather strength," said Eetoi. "Then I must return to the other world."

Earth Magician was silent, working at his loom.

Eetoi said, "There are many people here."

"But not too many!" said Earth Magician. "Everything here is as it should be!"

Eetoi agreed. "The men appear well formed."

"They are," said Earth Magician. "All of them can run and shoot."

"They look strong," said Eetoi.

"They are very strong," said Earth Magician, "and their hearts are good. They are properly respectful to an old man."

Eetoi smiled. "You speak as if they are the best people ever made."

"They are," said Earth Magician. "I have had much experience making people."

"Let me take them with me," said Eetoi. "Let me lead them to the upper world."

"No," said Earth Magician.

Eetoi told him, "My people want to destroy me. Four times they have killed me."

Earth Magician tied off a thread and said nothing.

"They had no reason," said Eetoi. "There were a few pranks, some jokes, but I am not an old man to sit on the mountain doing nothing."

"Old men are not idle when they sit," said Earth Magician. "They gather wisdom."

"That is why I have come," said Eetoi. "You are wise and skillful. My people are disrespectful. They must be driven from the land. Only your people are stronger. Only your people can fight them and win."

Earth Magician said, "My people have no war arrows."

"I will find quartz and help chip arrowheads," said Eetoi.

"War arrows must be fletched with eagle feathers."

Eetoi said, "Surely your men are strong enough to hunt and kill the eagle."

Earth Magician had many reasons why his people could not go. Eetoi found an answer to each.

"So it is," said Earth Magician. "They will go."

"There is much to do," said Eetoi. "Each man must have two pairs of sandals, one to wear and one to carry, eagle feathers for his headdress, red and black paint, extra bowstrings, twenty arrows tipped with quartz, cornmeal ground to mix with water. Bows must be strengthened, war clubs made."

Four months they prepared for war.

When all was ready, Earth Magician asked Gopher to

dig a tunnel, wide and winding to the world above. Eetoi followed. Behind him walked the men. Their hair was bound up, the parts painted red. Eagle feathers circled their heads. Their arrows were tipped with quartz. They were going to meet the enemy.

Coyote was going home at dawn. He saw a movement of the ground and stopped to watch.

The ground heaved and swelled. Gopher appeared, pushed aside the earth. Behind him came Eetoi, eyes painted black, a war club in his hand.

"I have come to kill Buzzard," he told Coyote.

Then he led the men from the Underworld. One after the other they came, popping out like ground squirrels and peering about. They looked so funny, Coyote laughed, and when he laughed, the hole shut. Eetoi was in the upper world and not all his warriors could follow.

"It does not matter," Eetoi told the men. "I have songs of magic, words of power. Though we are few, we will win!"

They had come up at the eastern rim of the world. Singing, Eetoi led them west. His enemies ran before them.

Men, women and young people fled. Only the old and very young remained in the little villages. Eetoi came and captured them.

Along the river, in larger villages, men prepared to fight.

With clubs and bows, they went to meet Eetoi. When they
fled, the battle ended. They left the dead, the old ones, the
wounded. Women and children were left behind. All were
captured by Eetoi.

Far to the west was the largest village, a village with
a great magician. Those who had fled were gathered there.
Buzzard hung above it.

"He comes," warned Buzzard. "Eetoi comes!"

The magician took soot from the council fire and blew
it into the air. Darkness spread over the land. It hid the
village. It hid the men who crept from it to surprise and
fight Eetoi.

"Where is the enemy?" said Eetoi's warriors. "Which
way do they come?"

Eetoi sang of the winds, the winds that had gathered
his flesh and bone. From south and east the winds answered. They broke the darkness and carried it away. The
men from the village were discovered. Eetoi's warriors
shouted. Arrows flew. The clubbers rushed forward.

Eetoi fought to the village, past the wall, to the meeting
ground. He seized the magician's hair, pulled down his
head and clubbed him. Buzzard he held by the neck.

"Don't kill me," said Buzzard.

"You had Sun kill me," said Eetoi.

"But you live," Buzzard told him. "Let me live, too. I'll

sing of you at the feast. Take my scalp and I'll dance with it, dance and sing of your victory."

Eetoi cut the skin around Buzzard's neck and pulled it off with the feathers. Buzzard's head and neck were left bloody and bare, bare and red forever.

The scalp was hung on a pole. When old women danced with enemy scalps, Buzzard danced among them. He carried his scalp and chanted his song but Eetoi was not there to see.

He sat in a hut, fasting and bathing, with only an old man to watch and chant. Those who had killed were carriers of power, a danger to the people. Each sat apart, alone except for an old man, until sixteen days had passed and each was properly purified.

Then Eetoi returned to his people, the men he'd led from the Underworld.

They had built new houses of poles and thatch so the breeze could blow through and the smoke could get out. They knew nothing of songs and ceremonies, and Eetoi began to teach them.

He gave them words and songs of power, songs for growing corn and curing illness, words of magic to find the enemy, ceremonies for calling rain. Like children, he taught them, then returned to Baboquivari. And his people settled near him at the center of the world.

Author's Note

Over fifteen hundred years ago an unknown people whom the Papago called the Hohokam, the Ancient Ones, arrived in southern Arizona, U.S.A., and northern Sonora, Mexico. They built irrigation ditches and multi-storied towns with clay walls. After a few hundred years they disappeared as mysteriously as they'd arrived.

The Pima and Papago say the Hohokam were driven away by their ancestors, led by Eetoi. Fifty years ago there

were still elders who could recite the names of the Hohokam ruins and describe the battles. But most archaeolo-
gists believe the Papago and Pima, or their ancestors, were
living in southern Arizona hundreds of years before the
Hohokam arrived. And they are still there, at the center
of the world.

They have changed, as have their myths. Both show
the mark of the white man's life and religion. Modern
collections of myths show little resemblance to those recorded almost a hundred years ago. They vary also from
village to village, from one anthropologist to another.

I've used the earliest recorded by anthropologists, com-
bining several versions or several myths. Also, I've added
portions of my own, a respectable practice since the
originals showed considerable borrowing from the Hopi,
pueblo dwellers in northeastern Arizona, as well as from
the people living westward along the Colorado River.

The myths were told in religious song cycles lasting
one or several nights. Song and narrative portions often
disagreed and there was much repetition. Four is a magic
number and four fours has the greatest power. Some songs
were sung sixteen times, whole stories repeated four times
with only details of color and directions changed.

I've simplified and modernized, but while reworking the

myths into a continuing narrative with modern story line, I've tried to keep the texture and truth of the very oldest originals, some of which are missing from modern collections.

But if stories are forgotten, Eetoi is not. The mountain peak of Baboquivari can be seen from almost any part of the Papago reservation near Tucson, Arizona. When the government requested permission to build an observatory on the peak next to Baboquivari, the Papago council delayed the decision for many months. It is said they were debating the effect on Eetoi, though he has not been seen for years, not since the railroad was built and he came down to herd the animals to safety.

NOVELS BY BETTY BAKER

Published by Macmillan:

Do Not Annoy the Indians

And One Was a Wooden Indian

A Stranger and Afraid

Published by Harper & Row:

The Shaman's Last Raid

Killer-of-Death

The Treasure of the Padres

Walk the World's Rim

The Blood of the Brave

The Dunderhead War